AT TAYLOR'S PLACE

AT TAYLOR'S PLACE

by Sharon Phillips Denslow

illustrated by Nancy Carpenter

Bradbury Press • New York

A special thanks to my neighbors Jim and Sherrie Fields
for their advice and the loan of their whirligig,
and to Sherrie's dad, George Chambers, who made it

—S. P. D.

Bradbury Press
An Affiliate of Macmillan, Inc.
866 Third Avenue, New York, NY 10022
Collier Macmillan Canada, Inc.

The text of this book is set in Monticello.
The illustrations are drawn in pastel.
Book design by Julie Quan

Printed and bound by South China Printing Company, Hong Kong
First American Edition
10 9 8 7 6 5 4 3 2 1

LIBRARY OF CONGRESS CATALOGING-IN-PUBLICATION DATA
Denslow, Sharon Phillips.
At Taylor's place / by Sharon Phillips Denslow ; illustrated by
Nancy Carpenter. — 1st American ed.
p. cm.
Summary: Tory helps her friend Taylor with projects including a weathervane
for Miss Perry, topped with a carved figure of her dog Marvin.
ISBN 0-02-728685-1
[1. Weathervanes—Fiction.] I. Carpenter, Nancy, ill.
II. Title.
PZ7.D433At   1990
[E]—dc20   89-23898   CIP   AC

To Em and Carroll
and the cousins next door
and to
Grandmother Riley
who taught me how to make a peach seed basket
and to
Granddad Riley
who gave me the pocketknife to carve with
—S.P.D.

To Lynn and Whit
—N.C.

On a cold fall afternoon, Tory puts on her coat and hat and boots and tromps over to Taylor's place.

Millie waves from the steamed-up kitchen
window of the farmhouse and cracks the window
open to yell, "Your mama and little Ben doing
okay today?"

"They're fine," Tory answers.

"Well, that's good. Taylor's out back."

Tory waves and follows the path under the
maple trees to Taylor's workshop at the back of
the farm.

The smoke from the chimney curls down to
welcome her. Then Taylor and Moustache are there
and Tory is inside.

It is like being in a snug cavern in the heart of the woods
at Taylor's place. The smell of the wood is everywhere—the clear
sharp smell of just-shaved wood curls, the deep seasoned smell
of stacks of wood waiting, the warm smudged smell of
charred wood in the old stove.

In the place of honor today is the weathervane for Miss Perry that Tory and Taylor have been working on.

There is nothing on top of the weathervane yet.

"Did you get him finished?" Tory asks.

Taylor points at the carved dog on the workbench. "Pretty near. He just needs a basket."

Tory runs her fingers around and around the smooth curves of the dog.

"He looks just like Marvin," she says, laughing.

"The ugliest dog in the world," Taylor says,
grinning back at Tory.

"Miss Perry will love him," Tory pronounces.

"It's your turn now," Taylor says. And Tory takes her special knife and carton of peach seeds and starts to work, carefully scraping a seed just as Taylor taught her. Soon a basket and handle take shape.

When she is finished, she slips a thin strip of leather through the handle of her basket and ties it around the dog's short neck.

Carefully Taylor glues and pegs the dog to the top of the weathervane.

"We make a great team," he says, stepping back to admire it.

Tory holds the weathervane on her lap as she
and Taylor head down the road to Miss Perry's
house in Taylor's old truck.

Miss Perry and Marvin come out to watch the
weathervane go up on a fence post at the edge of
the yard. Marvin has on a red sweater that matches
Miss Perry's red socks.

Miss Perry holds Marvin up to look at the carved dog. "Isn't it cunning, Marvin?" she says.

Marvin sniffs obediently at the wooden dog, then shivers in the cold and sneezes.

"It needs something," Miss Perry says, and she hurries back inside the house.

When Miss Perry comes out again she still has Marvin, but instead of wearing two red socks, she is wearing a red one and a purple one. In her hand is a piece of the other red sock.

She pushes the piece of sock over the little wooden dog so that it has on a red sweater just like Marvin's.

"There!" she says, and they all laugh at Marvin and Marvin in their matching red sweaters.

Tory and Taylor take the long way home, stopping at Taylor's barn to feed his goats and to fill the six bird feeders he has set up around the barnyard.

From their safe perches in the big maple, the chickadees and the titmouse family chirp and scold Tory to hurry.

It is growing late so Tory will have to start home soon, but first she and Taylor want to plan their next project.

Millie has been by Taylor's place, leaving them thick hot chocolate and a crackling fire.

The cats and rabbits and horses and pigs and dogs and goats and birds that Taylor has carved are silhouetted against the windowpane. Around each of their necks is one of Tory's peach seed baskets.

Tory and Taylor start working on a bluebird house for Mr. Hicks, but it is soon dusk and Tory has to go.

The smell of woodsmoke follows her, and as she hears the papery leaves rustle in the cold air, Tory imagines the little wooden dog with his basket and red sweater twirling around to meet the changing wind.